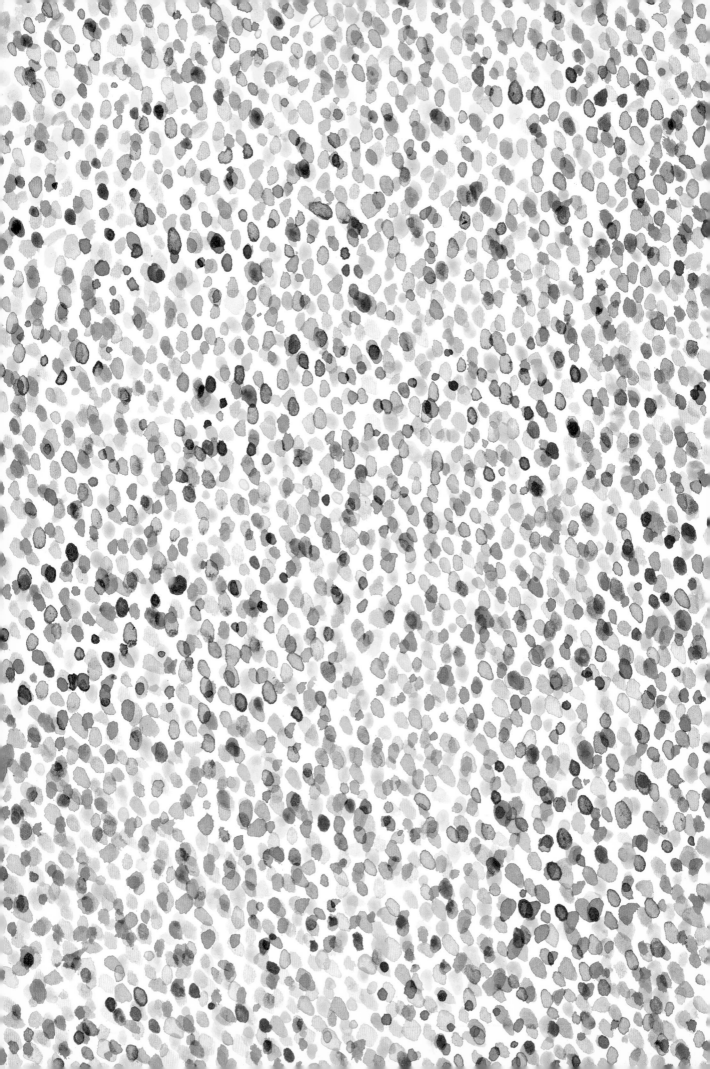

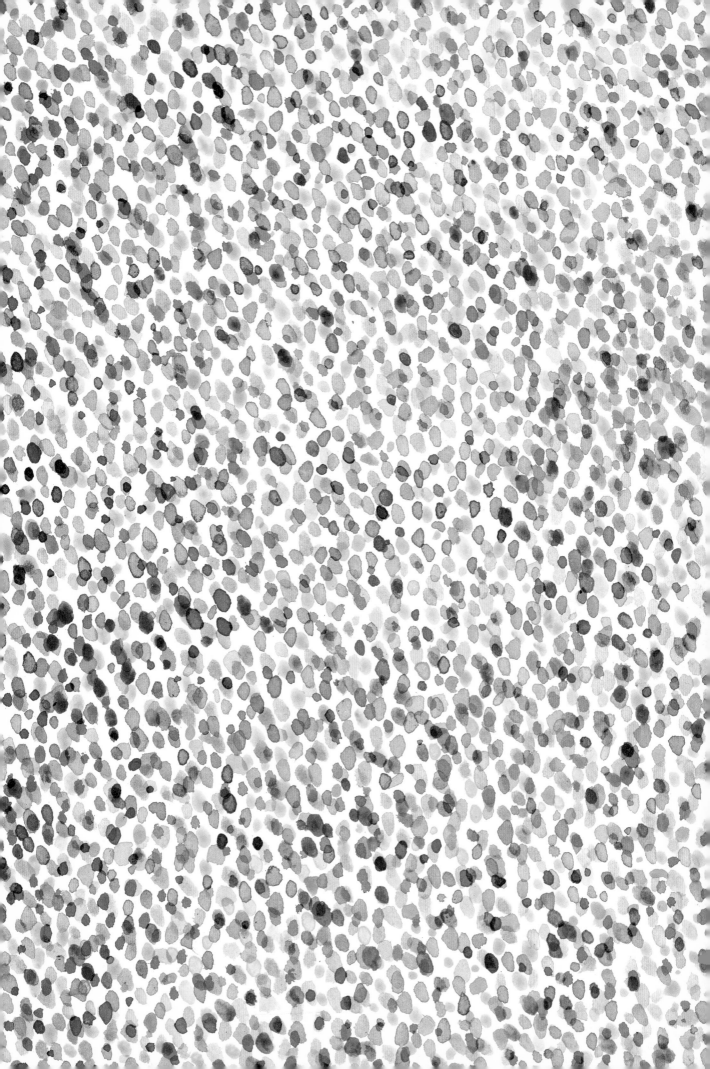

For Clinton and Clifton

ISBN 0-590-44453-0

Copyright © 1990 by Eric Carle Corporation.
All rights reserved. Published by Scholastic Inc.,
730 Broadway, New York, NY 10003, by arrangement
with Picture Book Studio.
BLUE RIBBON is a registered trademark of
Scholastic Inc.

12 11 10 9 8 7 6 5 4 3 2 1   2 3 4 5 6 7/9

Printed in the U.S.A.   08

First Scholastic printing, November 1992

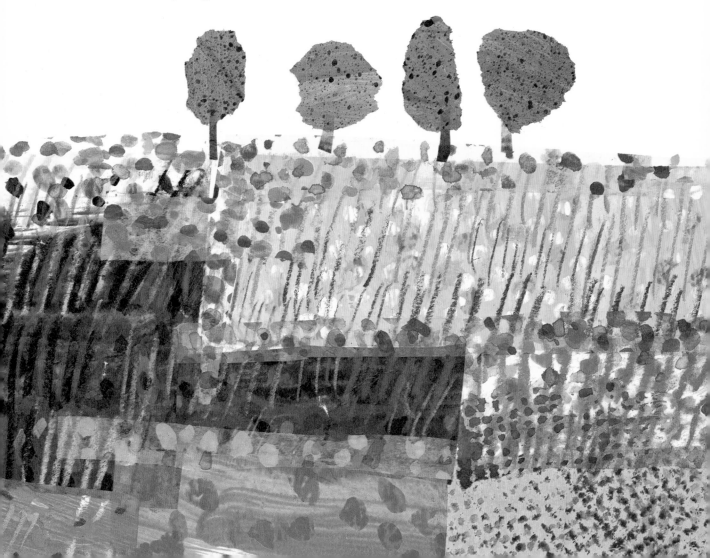

Pancakes, Pancakes!

Scholastic Inc.
New York Toronto
London Auckland Sydney

Kee-ke-ri-kee

crowed the rooster.
Jack woke up, looked out
the window and thought,
"I'd like to have a
big pancake for breakfast."

Jack's mother was already up and busy.
"Mother," said Jack, "I'd like to have a big pancake for breakfast."
"I am busy and you will have to help me," she said.
"How can I help?" asked Jack.
"We'll need some flour," she replied.

"Take a sickle and cut as much wheat as the donkey can carry.
Then take it to the mill. The miller will grind it into flour."

When Jack had cut enough wheat,
he put it on the donkey's back and took it to the miller.

"Can you grind this wheat for me?" he asked.
"I need it for a big pancake."
"First we must separate the grain from the chaff," said the miller.

He gave Jack a flail and spread the wheat onto the ground.
The miller took another flail and began to beat the wheat with it.
Jack helped with the threshing,
and soon there was a big pile of straw and chaff–
and a small pile of grain.

The miller poured the grain on a large flat stone.
On top of it was a round millstone
connected to the water wheel on the outside.
The water wheel turned round and round,
turning the millstone round and round, too,
to grind the grain into flour.
At last the miller handed Jack a bag of flour.

"Here's the flour," shouted Jack. "Let's make a pancake."
But his mother said, "Now we need an egg."
Jack went to the black hen and fed her some grain that had slipped
into his pocket while he had been threshing.
"Cluck, cluck," said the black hen and went inside the hen house.
Then she said, "Cluck, cluck," once more and laid an egg.

"Here's an egg," shouted Jack. "Let's make a pancake."
But his mother said, "Now we need some milk."
Jack went to the spotted cow and began to milk her.
"Moo, moo," said the spotted cow as the milk squirted into the pail.

"Here's the milk," shouted Jack. "Let's make a pancake."
But his mother said, "We need some butter."
Jack got the butter churn and held it between his knees.
His mother scooped the cream from the top of the milk
and put it into the butter churn.
Jack pushed the churn handle up and down, up and down.
Finally, the cream turned into butter.

"Here's the butter," shouted Jack. "let's make a pancake."
But his mother said, "We need to build a fire."
Jack went to the woodshed and brought some firewood.

"Here's the firewood," shouted Jack. "Let's make a pancake."
 But his mother said,
"Wouldn't you like to have something sweet on your pancake?"
 So Jack went down to the cool cellar
 and pulled a jar of strawberry jam from one of the shelves.

"Here's the strawberry jam," shouted Jack.
"Let's make a pancake."
In the kitchen, Jack's mother had filled the table with
the flour,
the egg,
the milk,
the butter.

There was also
a mixing bowl,
a cup,
a wooden spoon,
a ladle,
a frying pan,
a plate,
a knife, fork, and spoon.
And a jar of strawberry jam.

And his mother said, "Put a cupful of flour into the bowl...

"Break an egg into the flour and stir...

"Pour a cupful of milk over the flour and egg and stir again until the batter is smooth and without lumps."

Jack's mother heated the frying pan over the fire,
and added a piece of butter. The butter melted fast.

Then she said to Jack,
"Now pour a ladleful of batter into the hot pan."

After a minute or two she looked at the underside of the pancake.
It was golden brown.
"Now watch," she said, "I'll turn the pancake over. Ready?"

"Ready!" shouted Jack.
"Flip," said his mother.
Up and over went the pancake high into the air
and landed right in the pan. In another minute or two
the pancake was crisp on the underside as well.

Then she slipped the pancake from the frying pan onto the plate
and spread some strawberry jam on it.
"And now, Jack," his mother started to say,
   but Jack said…

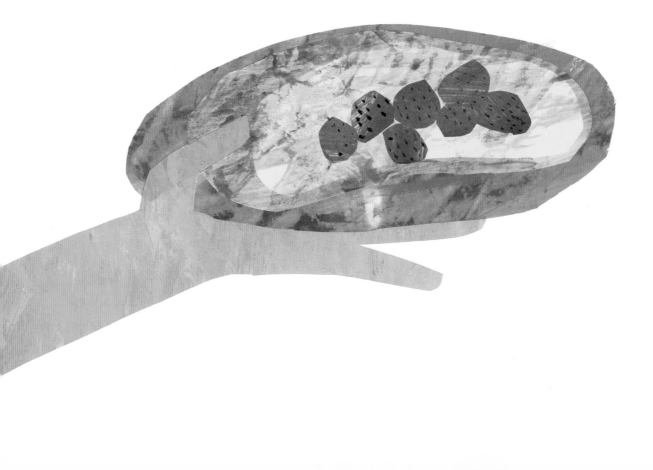

"Oh, Mama, I know what to do now!"

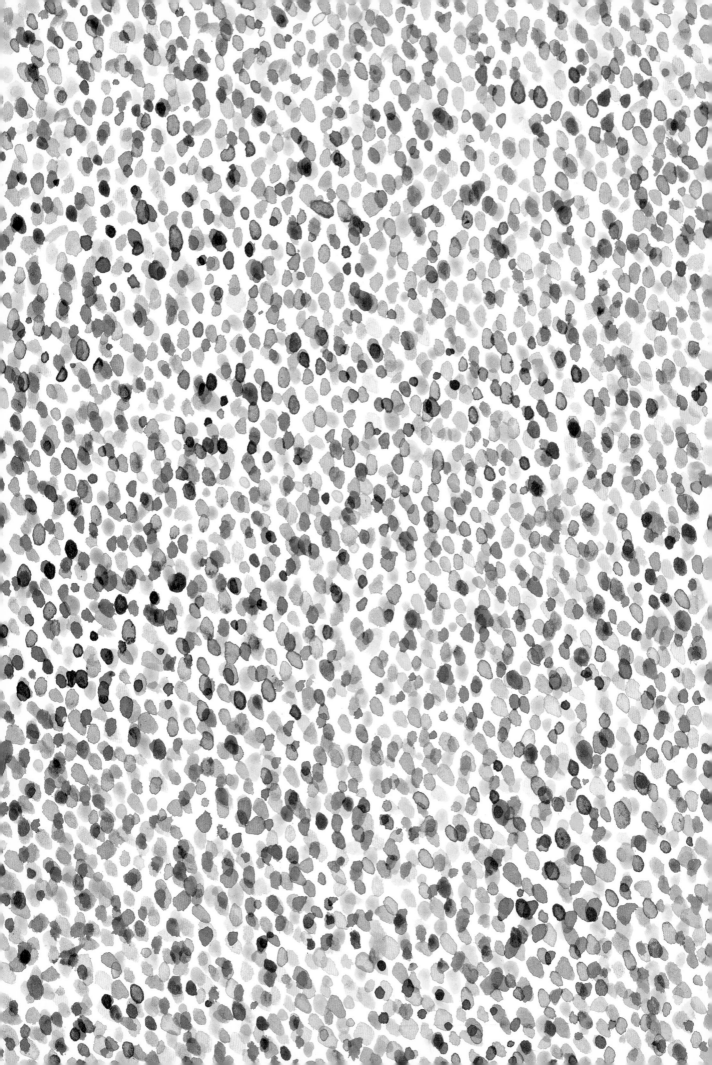

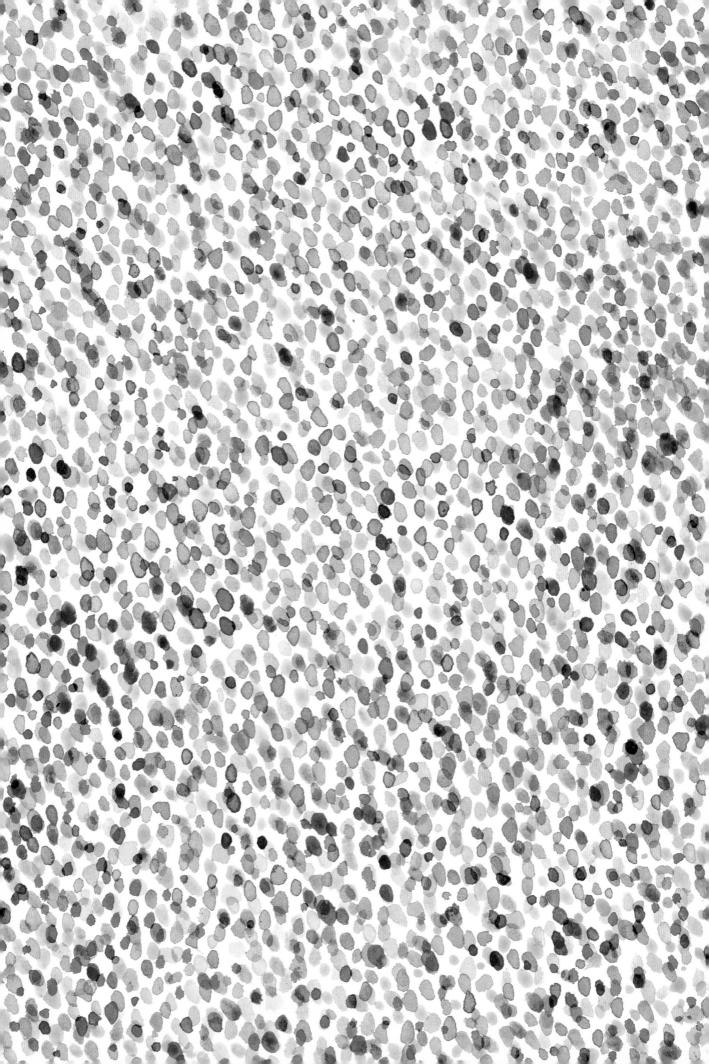